Journey To The Edge of the Mind
Take A Trip Down Queasy Street

Volume One
Eleven Tales of Fantasy

QUEASY ST

Written By Joe Alaskey

Best Selling Author of "That's Still Not All, Folks!!"
Voice of the ID Network's "Murder Comes To Town"
Emmy Award Winning Performing Artist

Packaged & Edited By
K.P. Lynne & R.J. Modell

Award Winning Best Selling Authors

Queasy Street
Volume One

Eleven Tales of Fantasy

Written By
Joe Alaskey

Packaged & Edited By
K.P. Lynne & R.J. Modell

ISBN#: 978-0-9971018-0-5

Hash Tag #Publishing

Words of Art
Hashed Between 2 Covers

Queasy Street Road Map

The Ogre
The Telling of Weird Tales Has Had A Long and
Revealing History, As In The Dark Ages...

Bugbear
When You're A Child, The Boogeyman Can
Seem Very Real, Sometimes It Is...

Force of Habit
As The Saying Goes, Some Men Are Born Great,
Others Achieve Greatness, and Some...

Peek-A-Boo
Reflect Upon This Particular Happenstance, You Can
Probably See It Coming...

End of Autumn
Sometimes One Can Get Carried Away With The
Spirit of Seasonal Change...

Lost and Found Again
Ever Dream About Your Past? What If Instead of Your
Going Back...

The Man With The Beaver Hat
Here's A Personal Fantasy I Couldn't Help But
Express Before It Crumbles...

The Trick and The Treat
Nothing Like A Nice Little Scare On Hallowe'en...

Holy Terror
Some People Are Never Satisfied, There's One In
Every Family...

Toupee or Not Toupee
While You're At It, Be Careful What You Don't Wish
For...

Daughter of Memory
People Enjoy Watching Films For Many Different
Reasons, Some Very Different...

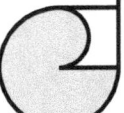

Introduction

By K.P. Lynne & R.J. Modell
Best Selling Authors

The short stories nestled in between these covers were selected for their fascinating form, taunting, whimsical and provocative use of grammar, and daring, cutting-edge style. Joe Alaskey is an enticing and tantalizing writer for the ages, a gifted wordsmith and a literary artist in every meaning and sense of the word. The first of four fascinating volumes, *Queasy Street: Volume One, Eleven Tales of Fantasy* will whisk you away into mysterious places and eclectic spaces where you have previously not been inclined to wander. So go ahead, we dare you! Take a journey to the edge of the mind and take a trip down *Queasy Street!*

The Ogre

The motley-clad jongleur slung his lute across his back and absorbed the happy, excited applause of the urchins for whom he had just sung about the elephant and the mouse, and got them laughing again in his practiced manner as a clown.

"Children, children, please! One at a time, please!" he feigned upsetment. "I have lots of stories and songs, and funny faces and --" His hands fluttered to his ears. "No, no, please! Oh, my poor ears!" he wept comically. "And now you're all laughing at me! Laughing! Oh, dear, dear me!"

Then he burst into laughter himself and sat upon a flat rock alongside the cobblestone road. He loved them so, the dear ragamuffins, loved to entertain them, but loved even more to teach them through his stories. And he knew they loved to learn, loved this part most of all. His little audience clustered around as he motioned for them to do so. Then, with a finger to his lips, they imitated him with choruses of "Shush! "Hear, now! Hear me now...! What kind of a story would you have? A funny story?"

"No!" they admonished, having only just heard one.

"No?! What, then?"

"A scary story!" piped several boys, remembering the street clown's past visitations.

"A what?! In the middle of the day?!" teased the jongleur.

"Yes!" exclaimed the ragged lads, hopping and clapping to the girls' doubtful dismay.

"Well, I do have a story about... an ogre!"

The children shivered with anticipation.

"But, what about a story of courage too? -- No? Ah, but what if it's the same story?" he prompted.

"'The Ogre'! Tell us 'The Ogre'!" the older boys shouted, the ones who had heard it before.

"Aha, yes! So that's the one you want? 'The Ogre'?"

The children generally agreed.

"Very well, then! Gather closer! Gather all 'round now! Little ones up front...! Shush now! Shush...!"

Some sat at his feet as his shushing echoed anew. Then, when all were quiet, he began:

"Now you might think this is just a made-up story about an ogre, because you know there are really no real ogres walking about. But once --! Once there *was* an ogre -- a real, live ogre! And *I know* because I *saw* him...!

"Well, I'm not sure if he were an ogre after all... but that's what the people of the little walled village called him.

3

"I first glimpsed him as I came to the gate of a walled village not far from here, some years ago. Before some of you were born, to be sure!

"He was up in a tree, picking apples! And as soon as he saw me, he hid...! Yes, among the branches of the tree!

"He was very oddly shaped, I must admit, and gave me quite a start! His head was somehow joined to his shoulders and he was hump-backed!"

Two little girls hid their faces.

"Oh, yes...! And even worse, he had no neck and no jaw, which made his mouth a wide slash and his body like a barrel, though his limbs were slender and strong!

"And for some other reasons, Nature had made him an albino! Yes, all white skin, and hairless from head to toe! Yet he looked to be only about... nineteen years, I'd say.

"When I reached the village tav-- eh, center of town, I told some of the residents what I saw and asked who he was. These people called him a monster. They told me all about him.

"When he was born, they said, his appearance brought his neighbors such fear and shame that they all moved away! But before he was nine months old, the town fathers insisted his family move into the woods beyond the South Wall of the village. His father had to give up his livelihood as a tailor and become an apple farmer. The villagers treated his parents badly and wouldn't even let their son inside the village walls to help sell the apples -- he was that ugly to them!"

The children's faces were now masks of pity.

"But, inside, he wasn't a monster at all!" he assured them. "*Or* an ogre...!"

Inside, he felt sad that after his parents died, no one ever called him by name, because no one had ever cared to ask what it was. Oh, they had a name for him, all right! But it was such an awful name that no one ever dared tell him what it was, so he never even knew.

"But he knew how they feared and hated him. And still his only wish was that someday, he could once again be within the walls of the village he knew and loved..."

So quiet they were, listening.

"Well, the day I was visiting -- just this past spring -- there he was in his orchard, picking apples to trade with the boys from the village market, -- when he saw some soldiers -- who were not of their army! -- hiding near the South Gate!"

The little ones held their breath; the boys grinned and eagerly looked at each other.

"Now I wasn't there with him, mind you, but this is what we all thought was the way it must have happened.

"After he heard these strangers whispering, he probably crept in closer and saw that they were Saxons, the deadly enemies of our regent! And then he must have heard them say that the little village was about to suffer a ruthless Saxon siege! -- planning to attack the West Wall...!"

The boys muttered amongst themselves.

"Hearing this, -- and without even thinking about it, -- the so-called ogre knew what had to be done...!

"All the rest, my children, is fact...!

"He then leapt upon his steed! And sped toward the South Gate, which was just starting to open! He rode past the astonished boys from the market who came for his apples, into the village he remembered and loved, for the first time in a long time, and right down the streets in broad daylight!

"The villagers were shocked at the sight of him, to say the least, but grew even *more* shocked to hear him shout a warning to all about the impending battle! Some didn't hear him at all and threw stones at him as he rode past them! And some didn't even know he *could* talk!

6

"Now, the Saxons were mere moments from their first foray of fiery arrows when the supposed monster and outcast reached the inside of the West Wall and climbed up in a trice! In plain view of all, -- including my humble and very frightened self! -- he stood, waving to the villagers, rallying them to gather and unite there to fight the invading Saxons as piercing, flaming death flew all about him!"

Many of the attendant youths were leaning forward, blinking and open-mouthed.

"I'd never seen such a sight in my life! It was inspiring, and finally spurred the confused villagers to action!

"As he turned to face the enemy, the brave apple-picker was struck in the chest with a flaming spear!" Gasps escaped from looks of horror.

"And though he staggered and fell back, his strength -- and especially his courage -- kept him high aloft the wall, urging the villagers onto battle!

"As he turned to face the enemy, the brave apple-picker was struck in the chest with a flaming spear!"

Gasps escaped from looks of horror.

"And though he staggered and fell back, his strength -- and especially his courage -- kept him high aloft the wall, urging the villagers onto battle!

7

"'The ogre! Fight with the ogre!' his former enemies cried! And how the battle raged -- with the bodies of villagers -- and especially Saxons -- falling like raindrops!

"Then, after a titanic and bloody struggle, the little walled village held fast and won the day...!"

Not a muscle stirred.

"But when the smoke of war was lifted, the brave and forgiving ogre laid dying, felled by a catapult, at the base of the West Wall. We drew closer to him...

"'My wish has finally been granted...'" he said.

"'You wished for death?'" I asked.

"'To die within these walls,'" he replied. The girls, and some of the boys, began to weep.

"The regent's cavalry sent for a physician, but they were too late, so the now-safe but saddened people of the little village buried him just where he fell..."

"I'll bet they were sorry now!" one older girl surmised.

"Yes, lass, they now understood that the ogre was their hero and that he had saved them even though they had all rejected him his whole life long. Some of them only knew him by the awful nickname they had given him, but now they said even that name with reverence."

"Because he had proven that even though his *outer* shell was indeed frightening, *inside, he was good... good as gold!*"

"He was *so* good that as they gently put him in the ground, inside the walls that were so dear to him -- at that very moment! I was inspired, --!" The storyteller deftly swung his instrument before him. "-- moved to write in dedication to him *this* humble verse..."

The boys and girls watched and listened carefully as the minstrel strummed a minor chord, and he sang:

"Humpty Dumpty sat on a wall...

Humpty Dumpty had a great fall...

All the king's horses and all the king's men...

Couldn't put Humpty together again."

By now, the sun was setting and suppers were cooking. The jongleur could smell them, so he dispersed the youngsters as he always did, with these words, "And remember, children, never forget...never forget!"

And somehow he knew they never would.

****

Bugbear

Theo had wandered into Daddy's den while Daddy was on the phone. Daddy was talking to someone about his grown-up business and he said something that Theo didn't understand. Theo was just four years old, so there was a lot he didn't understand yet.

"Ooh!" Daddy said to his faraway friend, patting Theo's head, "That'll be our *real* bugbear. We'll have to stop that right away."

When Daddy was done talking on the phone, he asked Theo what he was up to today.

"Daddy, what's a 'bugbear'?" asked Theo.

"Well! That's a good question, isn't it?" Daddy replied. "Let's go look it up in the dictionary! You remember what that is?"

Theo nodded. Then they walked to Daddy's little office together and Daddy opened the big book.

"Bugbear," he said as he flipped some pages. "Let's see. '"Buffy, bug, bugaboo, bugbane, bugbear'. Here we go. It says…" Daddy hesitated, reading to himself. "Hmm. It says it can be something like a big problem you have to solve… or… the boogeyman."

Theo thought and said, "Oh." Then he asked, "What's a bugaboo?"

12

"Same thing."

"Oh…"

Daddy didn't tell him what the dictionary said about it devouring little children. But he did tell him once not to be afraid of the boogeyman, because he isn't real. 'No such thing' he taught him."

"That's a bugbear?"

"Yes, son. That's what a bugbear is. But for me it's just a prob…"

"*That's* what's not a bugbear is!" exclaimed Theo.

"What do you mean, Theo?"

"Can we catch a bugbear and lock him up?"

"No, son. It's just make-believe. Don't worry about it. Remember? There's… "

"…no such thing," they said together.

Then Daddy left to use the bathroom.

Theo stood still by the big desk and said to himself: "That's not what a bugbear is! *I know* what a bugbear is! And I'm gonna find him and catch him!"

In a minute, Theo was at the kitchen table and took the jar of honey with both hands to his bedroom. Then he put the honey on the window sill while he fetched his teddy bear from atop his bed.

"Bears like honey!" Theo said to Teddy. "And *bugs* like honey too!"

Theo took Teddy to the window and opened the jar. Some honey spilled and trickled down the outside of the house. But he poured most of the honey right over Teddy, who was sitting on the window sill.

Then Theo took the honey-covered Teddy through the house, out the back door to the big tree outside his window. He set him down on an old tree root and watched. He watched as the ants and some other bugs came crawling over to get some honey. It took a while for enough bugs to come, and Theo helped some of them get there by pushing and carrying them along, until Teddy was covered with honey-stuck bugs. "*Now* you're a *bug*bear, Teddy!" Theo said, pointing at him.

Next he went back to the kitchen, got one of Mommy's dish towels, went out to the tree again and wrapped the bugbear in the towel. Then Theo carried the bugbear he made back into his bedroom, placed it carefully into his big toy box, and closed the lid.

"No more bugbear! I catched you and locked you up! So the boogeyman won't scare me anymore!"

But, Theo didn't bother to tell Mommy or Daddy what he did. He just went to bed very quietly that night because it was his secret.

As he was falling asleep, he thought maybe tomorrow he should tell them so *they* won't have to be afraid of the boogeyman anymore either!

Soon, Mommy and Daddy looked in on their sleepy son. They saw him cuddle with his stuffed giraffe.

"That's new," whispered Mommy. "I wonder where his teddy bear is…?"

"Theo? You still awake?"

"Yes, Daddy."

"Where's your Teddy, son?"

"Oh, I catched the bugbear and locked him up in my toy box!"

"But, Theo, --"

"Why did you do that, honey?"

"So the boogeyman can't get me or you or Daddy anymore!"

Mommy went to the toy box and opened it up wide. She took out the towel-wrapped Teddy, looked inside and squealed: "*Oh! Bugs! All over it! What did you do? Is this my honey?*"

Just then, they all heard a noise outside, an animal noise. A *big*-animal noise! Mommy dropped the bugbear.

Outside, right next to Theo's window was a bear - a real bear! Attracted by the scent of spilled honey, it was busy licking the aluminum siding clean of it.

Then the bear discovered the still-open jar of honey on the sill and swiped it close to his face, his tongue greedily licking out the contents. "Who left that honey there?!" shouted Mommy, backing away from the window. Her yell made the bear drop the jar onto the bedroom floor. "Oh, no!"

Daddy didn't know what to do. But Theo did! He picked up the bugbear and threw it at the real one with all his might! It stuck to the bear's shoulder and made him back up a few feet... But the huge beast seemed happy with his unusually tasty prize and lumbered off, licking at it as he returned to the neighboring woods.

"No more bugbear and no more boogeyman!" Theo grinned. Then Mommy and Daddy took Theo into bed with them. "We'll have to get him a new teddy bear," Mommy murmured, drawing the covers over them all. "Yeah, okay," sighed Daddy. "But I bet this is the first time the boogeyman ever *saved* a little kid!"

****

Force

of

Habit

As he stepped off the trolley, a stiff, cold gust of wind, the last of winter, smacked against him. And having no overcoat, Vinny Krepke felt it, chilled to the marrow of his slight self. With a wince, he skipped to the boardwalk and stopped to shiver. And to look around. Force of habit.

Nobody he knew and nobody suspicious in sight. Good, good. He looked up at the old, familiar sign and smiled wanly as he pronounced its words: "Parag-gon Beach." He ambled onward toward the gate, trying to recall the last time he'd been here.

He must've been a kid. Yeah, he remembered it was some summer when he was maybe eighteen or nineteen. He summoned the ghosts of laughing, scrambling bathers and placid cuties soaking up the sun. He remembered the merriment and peace on these sands, and how he'd fled their sight when Janey failed to keep their date, leaving him stranded, pissed off, and feeling ridiculous in his oversized swim trunks, ludicrous red socks with sandals, and the flowered, flamingo silk shirt which had suddenly felt cheap.

He grimaced at the memory, telling himself he'd always looked foolish in a bathing suit. He let that thought wash away all the others with new waves of anger and trepidation.

With another glance around the sparsely peopled street, he entered the open gate.

"W-W-Well, dammit, I got n-nowheres else to go!" he quietly cursed. He couldn't go back to the hotel. He'd seen Ferdy there just inside the lobby door. And that meant Fat Moe Sgritti was looking for him. Which was bad -- very bad news. "Imagine him thinkin' I'd rat on them!" -- when all he'd done was finger the Hudson as the getaway car in the Mercantile Bank heist. "One car! Big deal!" But the bulls had traced the car's registration to Fat Moe. Vinny hadn't known it was his personally, so now he was on the lam. "J-J-Just my luck!"

He figured this was the best place to hide, this rinky-dink little beach, all closed up for the season.

"N-N-Nobody'd think of this place," he hoped. He scuttled down the crookedly grinning boardwalk till he could duck inside the jagged shadows of the old concession stands.

He observed the darkening horizon. Storm clouds? Big ones anyway, like grey ice cream. He shivered. "Dammit! What if it r-rains? A-A-And me without no coat!" Just his tan, easy-to-spot suit and green hat with the feather.

"This is like a f-frickin' target!" He stuffed it into a wire trash basket. "F-F-Five bucks down the drain!"

He couldn't help recognizing how lonely and scared he felt, and ran a sweaty palm across his forehead. He guessed he'd hole up here, though, at least for a while. He could shop for food nearby. Maybe a scarf. Good thing he had cash in his pocket. He'd have to leave Jersey, though, and soon.

He looked from one stand to the next, examining his prospects, testing their padlocks: "Hot Dogs", "Cotton Candy", "Ring-Toss". Not very inviting as a flop. What else? "Skill Shoot"? "Freezey Treats"? No... These were just cold, empty wooden sheds with faded names and promises, but they were the best he could do for now. He studied their façades, wishing absurdly he'd find within one some lost prize, a stuffed toy or banner, anything to appease his gnawing anxiety.

What was that one? The sign was so small, he couldn't read it till he got closer...

H. F. Denry

Healer

Not a sign. A shingle. Like a Wild West Dentist, and about as old. He liked the antique look of it. Could he steal it?

Then he heard a door pushed shut. He bolted away instinctively.

Vinny saw that the shack rotted almost visibly, but "by God, s-s-somebody's inside!"

Its windows must have been boarded up twenty years ago. The shingle swayed a bit with the wind off the water. Vinny read it again, then said to himself: "Healer! Hah! Phy-Phy-Physician, heal thys-self!" He paced a tight circle, casing these digs as a possible hideout. "Hey. No p-padlock," he discovered. So he moved in on it.

It was just a simple latch. The door was open, in fact. It pushed open easily, soundlessly. Vinny swallowed, eyed the vacant beach one more time, and entered.

It seemed unnaturally dark, like he was wearing sunglasses. All the corners were hidden in black.

He focused on the dim interiors... A table and two chairs that matched the exteriors. How cozy. No other doors...? What's this? A murky, red and black, sagging tapestry from God-knows-what century.

He knocked on the door. "An-Anybody home?"

"Yes."

Vinny jumped in place.

"Come in and close the door..."

He was still adjusting his eyes when the deep, nasal voice pierced the gloom. Startled, he was tempted to run. Where was the guy?!

Vinny flinched again as the tapestry bulged, then pleated to one side, admitting a small, hunched silhouette.

The old man coasted across the rickety room, attended by a refrain of creaks which might as well have been from him as from the uneven, slivery floorboards. He stopped behind the nearer chair, against which he braced himself before briefly casting his lackluster gaze upon this off-season customer.

Vinny exhaled deeply with an enlightened sneer and a twinkle of amusement. He'd fallen for it, all right.

"The door, please."

"Yeah, ok-okay, sure!"

Vinny Krepke pushed the door shut. He was reminded of the carnival's Spook House he'd walked through in his youth, when his Dad still had the farm, and steeled himself for another mild scare. Of course, he'd been threatened by the best since then, no lie, and even paid for his erstwhile nerve with a broken nose and two knife-wounds along the way. So this, he figured, was only good for a laugh. What the hell, this old fart was harmless, though he began to wonder if anybody else was back there.

The only light now came in thin streaks from between warps in the old wooden walls.

"N-N-Nice c-crazy house ya got, Pops. L-Let's have little light here, hah?"

"By all means," the old voice purred, and into the tawdry box of a parlor spread the sudden illuminance of an unadorned, hanging light bulb.

With an unfriendly curse, Vinny covered his eyes with both hands, then parted them to blink back shattered sight.

"Sorry to keep you waiting in the dark." The weary monotone held a tone of sarcasm which Vinny instantly hated. "I am Denry."

"Oh, f-funny man, hah?"

Denry was not in any way a funny man, so the question elicited a second deadened glimpse in his direction.

As Vinny's vision cleared, he saw a man of his own short stature, twice his age but with thick, striated, silver hair and a large, drooping face limned by grim sobriety. The eyes were ponderous drops of ice, a freezing stare mounted atop a still, slight frame hung with sackcloth.

Vinny frowned in assessment of this wrinkled, wooden wraith, spurting a snort of ignorance. "Wha-Wha-Wha-Wha-- What kinda healer are you anyways? What gives here?"

"You do, hopefully, in return for my services," Denry lowed.

"You hea-heal people, huh?"

"Yes." The voice was flat in tone and frankness.

Denry had studied him by now. The sickness was obvious. His twisted fingers beckoned. They sat.

Vinny leaned his elbows on the table, felt its level shift and retracted them awkwardly.

A mutual silence grew as Denry's grave probing met Vinny's narrowing lamps.

Held by childlike fascination and something unknown to him, Vinny sat in the hard old chair, engaged in what he took to be a preliminary staring contest. He goosed his head forward and widened his pale blue eyes in juvenile mockery.

Denry saw this need to belittle and scorn, but would not let his own countenance harden with disapproval. He needed to concentrate.

Seeing his antics were getting him nowhere, Vinny sat back and folded his arms.

"Hey, wha-what's with the silent treatment? You gonna ta-talk to me or what?!"

Denry dimmed his glare and sat back as if exhausted. "I am a healer. Therefore, you, my friend, have come to me for a reason. What is it?"

Vinny blinked in confusion, resentment swelling. "Ai-Ain't you supposed to have a crystal ball here, swami?" He laughed, a silly, convulsive chuckle.

"It is not my function to entertain, my friend, but to cure," Denry uttered by rote. "Now tell me... What is your problem?"

For a second, Vinny thought of Fat Moe and Ferdy, but knew he couldn't have meant *them*.

This hesitation weakened his bravado, and Denry's face took a kindlier cast.

"Let me explain... In all my many seasons of endeavor, those of you who have crossed my threshold have wished to *fix* or to *cure* some unfortunate part of themselves... You are no exception... But you must clear your mind and choose, and tell me how I might help."

Vinny didn't know what to say.

"Tell me specifically what it is that you would have differently," Denry sighed. "Something you would change..."

"I-I don't get this. About myself, you mean?"

Vinny swallowed air.

"Yes, precisely."

25

"Well, I ain't g-g-got no diseases. I-Is that what you mean?"

Denry sat and waited. Vinny glowered back tensely.

"Well, c'mon, *c'mon!* Gimme a cl-cl-clue, will ya?! I ain't no good at g-g-guessin' games!"

Denry's slow shrug bore intolerable weight.

"You will not trust me... Go."

With this chilly rejection, Vinny slid up in his seat.

"Hey, wai-wai-wai-wait a minute! Okay, I get it! I know what you m-mean now! Y-Y-You don't fix no diseases. You fix o-other problems. P-P-Personal problems, right?"

The old sage saw the pain and unhappiness before him, touched gnarled fingertips to his well-furrowed brow, and took pity. Although he began to feel his own, much deeper pain regenerating within, pressing him closer to the brink he knew he must inevitably leap, perhaps even today. But if one more soul could be relieved...

"So you *want* to trust me after all," he said at length. "I don't take many customers nowadays. Times have changed, haven't they? Frivolous, fun-seeking tourists, callow adolescents, potential vandals and thieves... They've been my only trade of late. And I myself have grown rather... selective."

His inner voice warned him to withhold mentioning his poor health, his sense of nearing death.

"And advancing age has made me jealous of the power."

"Power...?" Vinny echoed. "Wha-Wha-What power?"

Denry closed his eyes.

"A-A-Are you a -- a whattyacallit? A hypnotist or somethin'?"

"No."

"A healer."

"Yes."

Vinny stroked his lower lip.

"So -- So you can solve my personal problems, right? And i-i-if I let you, you'll cure whatever problem I s-s-say. I got that right...?

"W-Well, I'll tell you right off the bat, Professor, I -- I wish to hell I di-di-didn't stutter so much!"

"Whatever it's worth to you, that's all."

Vinny's grin slithered back. If this was a snow, the old geezer was pretty damn good at it. And if it *was* on the level...

"Okay, Professor! So go ahead! M-Make with the power!"

The old eyes oozed open.

"Very well. Only, understand this --"

Aha! *The catch.* Vinny's eyebrows arched to the challenge.

"Once you have been healed, my responsibility ends. My work is guaranteed, so you will be cured, my friend. Then you will pay me what you like, and leave... Any questions?"

"Well, what if I o-o-only pay you a dollar?"

"Then you'll pay it and *leave. Immediately.*"

"A-A-And you get rid of this s-stutter... forever?"

"No. *You* get rid of the stutter forever."

"N-N-No tricks? No catch?"

"No... Do you accept my terms? Shall we begin?"

"You can rub out a ba-bad habit just like that, huh? How l-l-long will it take?"

"Bad habits are my specialty... It takes only a few moments. And once healed, it will be as if you had never stuttered at all." Denry knew what his answer would be, and stood with difficulty, as the agony in his chest held tight. "You understand, and agree to my terms?"

Vinny pulled at his lip again. What did he have to lose? Except one dumpy, drafty hidey-hole.

"Okay. S-S-S-Sure...!"

Denry moved from his chair; Vinny stiffened in his as the old man walked around behind him.

"Hey, wha-wha-wha--?"

"Please be quiet."

Vinny felt the old geezer hold his cheeks in his hands. They felt cool. His expression of distrust and reluctance was smoothed away. He shut his eyes.

But then a bubbling fire started on his tongue and he thought his mouth was being fused shut. He wanted to yell but his heart was muscling in on his throat. He tried desperately to get up but then there was a pop like his head had been yanked off. Denry let go. Vinny collapsed, shuddering aloud, face-first onto the table. He heard the slow panting behind him, but couldn't sit up and look just yet.

Vinny heard the healer hobble back around the table, and opened his eyes when the planks stopped groaning. The old-timer was gripping the back of his chair with whitened claws, the bare sticks-for-arms trembling. He opened his mouth to bawl the guy out, but found no real reason all of a sudden. He felt fine now. Better, in fact. So instead he said: "Is that it...?"

"Keep talking," Denry replied.

"Keep talkin'? Whattya mean? What for? You want me to just keep yappin' until I say somethin' interest--?"

It dawned on him now. "Hey, wait a minute here...! Hey, it worked! I'm not stutterin' anymore!"

Fatigue outfought the healer's perfunctory blessing.

Vinny Krepke leaped from his chair, astonished.

"Hey, Professor, you did it! You fixed me! Hey, listen to this! Listen to me! I don't stutter anymore!"

"Don't repeat yourself," Denry deadpanned.

Vinny laughed and bounded over to his benefactor, thanking him with an energetic handshake. So it felt cold again. So what? This old bastard knew his onions! And he was done with him anyway.

"Oh, this is terrific! You did it! How'd you do it?!"

Denry reclaimed his hand. "It was neither too easy nor too difficult, my friend. Now let us settle accounts."

"Okay, okay! Fine! Sure!"

Vinny swung his left foot up onto his chair, fished in his sock for the cash, and laid down ten, twenty, forty, -- fifty smackeroos.

"Betcha never saw green like that before, hah?"

"You'd be surprised what people leave, and what some will pay..." Denry stood, leaving the money on the table, not looking at anything, just gathering himself around his aching insides.

"Yeah? Well, it was worth it, pal, believe you me!" Vinny stood, grin fixed, wiping his hands on his jacket and starting to figure some sharp new angle.

Denry stood as tall as he could. "And now, if you would --?" The delicate hand gestured toward the door.

"Yeah, okay, sure. I'm leavin' now. Only -- You gotta tell me how you did this. 'Cause this was more than I expected, y'know?"

The old healer bowed his head. "You promised. Please. No more questions. You must leave."

Vinny vacillated. "Okay, pal. That's right. I'll be goin' now." He got halfway to the door.

"Hey, you all right? You need a doctor or somethin'?"

"Don't concern yourself!" the elder suddenly thundered. *"Just go!"*

Vinny bristled, his face crinkling rudely.

"Hey, that's not too friendly, my friend. Y'know what I mean, Professor? Here you just finished doin' me the favor of my life, and now you're hollerin' at me to take a powder! And here I am feelin' all sympathetic an' --"

Denry buried his face in his hands, quaking with pain. "Hey. Now just take it easy, all right?"

The old creep didn't even look up as he crossed back to him. "Look at you! You're all white and shakin', for God's sakes!" He took his elbow. "Whyn'tcha just siddown and --?"

"Take your hands off me, you fool!" Denry sizzled, the bitter words stinging like a slap.

"Okay, *sure!*" Vinny's temper flung the ancient, flaccid arm from his grasp. Denry stumbled, bracing himself against the wobbly table.

"Just tryin' to help you is all!" the fugitive griped.

"You are a liar," the healer stated blankly. "You said you would go immediately."

"But you need help, pal! Look, I can't leave you like this!" Vinny trumped up his case on the spot. "After what you done for me? No-sir-ee! You look like you're ready to croak, Professor! Now c'mon. Siddown."

Denry no longer refused his assistance. He merely slumped back in his chair, gaping vacantly. Vinny squatted next to him, still holding the arthritic fingers in his. Now all cylinders were clicking, all right!

"Hey, listen. You did me a great big favor, Professor. Now, I ain't gonna rob you or nothin'. *All's I wanna know... is how the hell you did it.*"

"Get out," the shaman murmured. "You are an evil little viper."

Vinny lashed out at the unmoving face, spilling the old man onto the floor. "You're dyin', you old bastard! You oughta pick your words more careful!"

"You are evil, but you are also right... I *am* dying."

"Vinny Krepke stood, disgusted. He wouldn't get anything out this rotten old creep now. Maybe he should cack him, if only to end both their misery.

But no, now it was his turn to take pity.

"I could say 'Good riddance,' y'old windbag. But I'm still grateful, see? Even if you insult my head off. Maybe I'll even call an ambulance on my way to..."

"I know what you want," the unexpected words drifted up. "You want the power... *Don't* you?"

It wasn't an accusation. It sounded to Vinny like an *appeal*. Like he *wanted* him to have it.

"It is the power to heal, my friend. To cure your fellow man."

"Take my hands..."

Vinny obeyed. His meat hooks were hot again, hot as hell.

"To the table... as before... Keep holding on..."

33

He obeyed each command.

"Close your eyes. And hold on tight ... no matter -- no matter what."

"*Now* who's repeatin' --?" he started to joke.

Denry tightened his feeble clasp till the bent bones squeezed like vises. "Jesus! The death grip!" Vinny's mind panicked silently as he rose to a crouch.

Then something like lightning sparked between them, and both parties shot apart with an explosive repulsion that sent them crashing against opposite walls...

Vinny's head, the only upright part of his body, leaning against the baseboard, lolled gingerly a few moments before he dared to sit up. He had to hold his neck and bat away the stars and neon squiggles.

"*What the hell was that?!*"

"The power is now yours," rasped the voice from across the room.

Vinny saw the old man crumpled there, both arms and maybe one leg broken. He crawled over to him.

"Mine now, huh? Does that mean --?"

"Use it. Use it now. Your hands..."

Vinny felt his neck again, massaged it, and healed it.

"Wow! You're right! I thought I busted my neck just now, but...now *I* got the power!"

He saw Denry try to move, try to ease his spindly, shattered limbs, and manage to choke out a single laugh, but with breath that was thinner, lighter now. "There's your proof...!"

Vinny got to his feet and eyeballed the old coot on the floor.

"Hey, thanks, Professor. Oh, I'd fix you up too, only I don't think you could afford it now."

"Oh, no. Don't bother... I wouldn't live through it anyway. My time is almost up."

"That's what I figured," Vinny nodded as he scooped up his fifty bucks from here and there. "We're even-Steven now, huh?"

Denry's eyes looked deader than ever as they started to slide shut.

"Well, so long. If you still want that ambulance, --"

The grey hands twitched limply. Not much of an answer.

Vinny Krepke strode to the door. First, he'd change his name --

"One last word, my friend..."

35

Vinny froze, turning on his heel, not daring to look.

"So there's a catch after all, huh? I knew it. *I knew it!*"

He made a beeline for him, throwing the table over in fear and frustration.

"Why, you old gleep! I oughta kick your false teeth in...! What is it?!"

"The conversion process."

"The wh-wh-what?! Wha-Whattya mean?!" He noticed the stutter was back. "H-H-Hey!' His eye ticced.

"It'll all be over in a year or so."

"Wha-Wha-What will?! What kinda process?!"

"I've already told you, my friend. Bad habits are our specialty," the ex-healer whispered with, finally, a smile.

Eventually, some kids on the other side of the fence heard the noises coming from the shack.

A cop called the ambulance. Two bodies were removed.

One was a twitching, knotted travesty of a man, a spastic, whimpering, frenzied wretch, lisping and stammering demands for a hundred jumbled appetites: a cigarette, some candy, some gum, a fix, booze -- beer, wine, whisky, gin! Anything! It twirled its forelock, bit at its fingernails, and wept.

The other was mercifully dead.

****

Peek-A-Boo

Oh, my ear! Miserable bitch! I've never itched so hard in my life!! What *is* it?!

And look at *this* now!! Bleeding? No. Pus? No, but *some*thing...!!

Something under there... A lump. A little lump. Splitting my ear open!! -- The cartilage, the skin -- pushing, throbbing -- on its way *out*...!!

God help me, what is it?

Oh! The itch! Ah, the pain!! Must be bleeding...! Just a little...

But the lump -- The little white lump is... *growing*...! *Growing...! Hideous bubble!! What are you?!*

Now I can see it... sticking out.

Revulsion.

And...a dot... A tiny, dark dot on it, in it... moving, making little circles now, widening, widening...! Growing! And... And... circling, focusing like a -- like an eye! *It's an eye...! An eye growing out of my ear! Why?! Why?!*

I'm not seeing things. It *is* there, and it *is* an *eye*.

It is not seeing things either, thank God. So far. That is, as far as I can tell.

But what if it does...?! It would distort my vision, show me three distinct images, one askew!

I'd probably go mad. Wait…Wait just a second now…

The eye… It is starting… to focus, to *see* --!! Out of the side of my head! I can see myself in the mirror on the left wall! -- looking at myself with my *new eye…!!*

God, this is *scary!!* What should I *do?!* Got to do *something!! But what?!*

See a doctor? Call one? Call Aja? Roger? Itaru? Mom? No, what could *they* do?? Stare and cluck with sympathy, that's all. Or tell me to start wearing a pirate patch.

Heh! It's crazy! Or *I'm* crazy!

An eye grew out of my ear, and… wherever I go, whatever I do, from now on, is going to be done by -- a freak. Unspeakable.

No, I know!

I can have it *removed…!*

Certainly! That's what I can do!

It's the *only* thing to do!

I'll find the right surgeon somewhere and show him the problem, and certainly he'll agree to remove it for me! I'll pay 'em whatever they ask! Just so I can return to normal.

Because -- a person is not supposed to just… grow eyes suddenly! Not where they don't belong…! Or anywhere else, come to think of it!

I hope it won't be painful. No, it's surgery. You'll be put under.

But it was so painful growing out...!

It's not the same thing at all. Relax.

Besides, how do you know any of this is real? Think one second. Weren't you asleep? Couldn't this be a dream...? In fact, *isn't it?!*

Ohhh! What was that...?

Oh... Just a dream. Thank God!

A dream? That was a nightmare!!

Growing another eye! Out of my ear! What a wild ride!

Had me going, all right!

Whew! I'm sweating!

And just look at me in the mirror over there! I'm a *wreck...!*

' -- over *there...*'?!

****

End

of

Autumn

Hot! Hot! Hot! Hot beyond belief! Hot beyond endurance! Damned summer! That's what he thought. Oh, well, it was almost over…this miserable heat. This damnable season. Crispin Frietchie hated the summer. He couldn't understand it. He couldn't see why others didn't hate it as much as he did.

Everyone was sweating, overheating, keeling over and even dying from it! Still, off they sped to the beaches. They couldn't wait to get even hotter! And brown and burn and broil themselves all in the name of fun! How asinine!

He was glad it was almost over, very glad. Soon the cool winds would return and the temperatures would drop, and he would be comfortable once again. But every year, he missed his walks outdoors. He couldn't walk in summer, just couldn't! All right, wouldn't. His middle-age spread made it difficult too.

To Hell with summer! He wasn't built for it anyway. He would watch the calendar and the thermometer and stay indoors with his air conditioning. And so he did. And soon the heat diminished, just as he knew it would.

Now all the ignoramuses were back indoors! Now he could finally open a window. He opened all his windows when the first cool New England evening arrived. And his thoughts began to cool with the breeze.

He looked around his sumptuous parlor. Now he could enjoy it again. His curtains could billow again. His paintings and statues could breathe again. And so could he. And now he could go outdoors and take his afternoon walk again.

Crispin Frietchie left the door open behind him when he finally went outside. "So his house could breathe," he chuckled to himself. No one lived within a mile of his estate anyway, so off he went on his leisurely stroll, breathing extra deeply, smiling to himself.

He checked the thermometer on the porch before he left. It was a nice, cool sixty-three degrees. At last, the colder weather had arrived, all in one blessed day. No need yet for his hat or scarf or his gloves, but he'd put them on anyway, because he wanted to.

"Oh, how I wish it could always be like this," he declared right out loud, watching the first brown leaf fall to the ground. "I would abolish summer forever and embrace the autumn eternal!" He felt poetic that day. "And autumn...autumn is bliss!" he further expounded to none but himself.

A couple of months later, it was nightfall by the time he returned from his walk. Almost all the leaves had fallen now, and, as usual, he had carefully avoided stepping on them.

Otherwise, the leaves would crackle and fragment beneath his tread, and this he didn't like. A stronger, much cooler breeze was blowing now and ushered him back indoors. Actually, he felt odd about that. The wind somehow felt like hands, gently pushing him into his house. He smirked at himself for that thought. But he locked the big door after he closed it, before pocketing his gloves and hanging up his hat and his scarf.

"Simpleton," he chided himself. "What have you to fear? You are wealthy, you are self-sufficient, and never lonely, with all your books and films and music and works of art around you. And no one wants to hurt you. You are safe here."

He'd never leave this house in the summer though, he reminded himself, to seek out cooler climes, although he could obviously afford it. He would feel uneasy away from home. He loved his house, loved staying in it all year round, no matter what. So he suffered through summertime, as usual.

And now autumn was nearing its end. He had six or seven more wonderful months to enjoy his singular life. And he would, and happily, too, with as little contact with anyone as humanly possible. With summer dead, buried and forgotten now, a lovely winter was approaching once again!

Crispin Frietchie went to a window and inhaled the cold air deeply. It was then that he thought he heard a peal of eerie, distant laughter. He frowned, more in puzzlement than annoyance. Who in the world was that? What a crazy laugh! Like a cartoon giggle, quite unreal! He shivered. On impulse, he closed the window.

"Idiot neighbors! Having a party? Well, good for you," he clucked to himself. "Even from a mile away, you people are a damn nuisance!"

He went over to his stereo console and played an LP, one of his collection of piano classics. *Autumn Leaves* by Ferrante and Teicher always made him smile. In a moment or two, he chanced to look back at the window he had closed.

And there, on the other side of it, a strange, grinning face was rocking back and forth, sunset eyes aglow with mischief! Crispin shouted with fearful surprise. He backed up into the console, and the record player needle bumped and screeched in shock athwart the vinyl surface.

Then, when he dared to look again, the crazy face was gone. He flew in a frenzy from window to open window, pulling them shut, locking each one tight. He was panting, panicked, perspiring as he went, though he could see the white plumes of his breath. And when he finished, he fell back against the wall.

"Who or what in the name of God was that?!" he exclaimed loudly. "A madman! A madman outside my window! Oh! That face!" The image wouldn't leave his mind. That crazy, bobbing head, shining eyes and toothless grin! Yes, he was toothless, except for one tooth. Old -- ancient! Insane! Head just rocking, rocking, to and fro, silently watching, grinning...! An old madman! Staring in at him!

And wasn't he wearing a hat -- an orange hat, by God?! Yes, a little orange hat! And a bright green shirt -- with red stains down the front! Ghastly!

Crispin Frietchie called the police. He spoke with a very calm, even-voiced Sergeant Haley, who asked him to describe the man at the window. So he did. And the Sergeant listened. And when he got to the part about the bloodstains and hat, there was a silence on the other end of the line.

Then Sergeant Haley said, "Mister Frietchie, the way you describe all of this, it sounds like someone's playing a joke on you." A joke?! Crispin didn't know what to say in response.

"This man was smiling, you say?" inquired the sergeant. "Yes, but -- no! Not smiling! Grinning, -- ear to ear! His mouth was closed, but I could see he had no teeth!"

46

"No teeth?"

"Yes, no teeth! Well, one tooth... But I could tell by his eyes --!"

"He was old, then?"

"Yes! Yes, he was very old! But there was this mad glint to his eye! And he was just rocking his head back and forth! Back and forth! He was crazy! He must be crazy, I tell you!"

"I see..." the sergeant sighed. "Well, it doesn't really sound like anyone who lives around this area."

"Well, maybe it doesn't! But maybe he's an escaped lunatic or something! And you can't tell me some old people don't dress exactly like that! Weird... bright colors! Or maybe...well... do you think I made all this up?!"

The next pause infuriated him.

"Well, do you?!"

"Uh, no, sir. But, Mister Frietchie, I don't mean to get personal about this now, but you are pretty well-known to people around town to be... a bit reclusive, sir?"

"Yes? Yes?! Well, so what if I prefer my privacy?!" Frietchie protested. "I'm telling you I saw a deranged old man peeking in at my window! Now are you going to do something about it or not?! And right now! Please, Sergeant Haley?"

He said "please" but it sounded rather unpleasant. And after another silence, the policeman said, "All right, we'll send someone out there. Just stay inside, sir."

"I will! I will!"

"And in the meantime, I'd suggest you lock your windows and doors."

"Well, of course! That's the first thing I did! And drew the curtains too! Just hurry, please, hurry! I'll wait! I'll wait..." They hung up, and Crispin Frietchie exhaled with a modicum of relief. But he still felt very alone and very frightened -- and in his own house no less! How unfair!

He ambled around the parlor and noticed that the stereo was still on, with the record still turning. He leaned down, turned it off, and looked sadly at the scratch on his album, as he put it back in its sleeve. He looked around once more and turned off the parlor lamp – and then turned it on again.

Then he listened closely for any noises outside as he walked to the staircase. He started climbing slowly. But he ran the last few steps. It was dark upstairs, he saw, as usual, so he put on the overhead light in the hallway before stealthily entering his room. It was dark in there too. And only one light, he now regretted, next to his bed.

48

He tried to swallow the dryness in his throat as he looked at the closed window just beyond it. He could see the moon a bit above the top of his birch tree, as usual, because he'd left the curtains open. He saw the emptiness of its up-reaching branches, waving, wanton in the winter wind.

He swallowed again and tiptoed toward the window, holding his breath and fighting the impulse to cry. He crossed the length of the room, stood next to the curtain, put his hand out and touched it to the stiff, red velvet...And there was the face again! The mad old man was back! So suddenly! And up so high! But how?!

And now he could see more! It was impossible, but ... he could see his tiny, weird body just floating there... floating! And this time, next to his bobbing, grinning head, the apparition held something long and thin and sharp!

Crispin Frietchie shrieked in the dark. Quaking and shrieking, he stumbled and fell against the bedpost and crashed to the floor. Words emerged through his shouts of horror, "No, no! Go away! You crazy old man! Crazy old man! Leave me alone!"

But he couldn't take his eyes off the window. And he couldn't, he couldn't stop shrieking as he watched the old head nodding back and forth, back and forth, disturbingly playfully! And then the old man laughed at Crispin, frightfully, mockingly...that same uncanny laugh he'd heard before! He saw his single tooth glistening as he twirled and whirled that long, sharp instrument, very fast! And now he was moving closer to the window!

Sergeant Hadley read the report in the presence of the officers on the scene. They had to break in, they officially wrote. They really had no choice. The door to the Frietchie house had been locked, and it was a strong old oaken one, so one of them had to go in through a window, then open the door for his partner.

In the meantime, they heard this crazy laughter coming from upstairs. So they pulled their weapons and proceeded to investigate the goings-on. But they holstered their weapons after entering the bedroom. Because that's where and when they found Mr. Frietchie, in the dark, on the floor, laughing hysterically. Laughing, apparently, at nothing at all.

"He couldn't stop laughing," the sergeant read. "He was just laughing and pointing at the window." They tried to get him to talk to them, but he just wouldn't or couldn't stop laughing.

"So, a few minutes later, we decided to call St. Andrew's. We stayed with Mr. Frietchie until the E.M.s arrived. They diagnosed shock, sedated and secured him, and then they took him away. They also told us they'd probably have him under observation awhile."

And that was the end of the report. Sergeant Haley sat back and looked at his men, a slight frown clouding his brow. "Did you search the premises? Look around outside for footprints near the windows?" he asked.

"We did, Sergeant," one replied. "Nothing there."
"You should've put that in your report," he said as he tossed it back at them.

"Yeah, you're right. Sorry..."

The officers waited. A moment later, the sergeant's brow creased philosophically.

"So the fat little hermit was nuts after all. He sure sounded like it when I talked to him... How's he doing today?"

"In fact, they called. They said he's still laughing..."

"Well, maybe he'll stop eventually. And you say he was pointing at the window?"

"The one in his bedroom, right."

"On the second floor?"

"Right. The second floor."

The little frown returned.

"What was he pointing at? You saw nothing unusual?"

"No, sir. Just a tree."

"A tree, huh?"

"Just a birch tree... That, and a touch of frost on his windowpane..."

****

Lost

and

Found

Again

"Oh, good. The rain is stopping," she observed, just before crossing the street.

Lindy Shelby, thirty, blonde, plain but always pleasant, was on her way home after brunch with some of her friends from the Senior Center who, like her, volunteer their spare time and energies to help others in need.

Ross remained unimpressed but tolerant of his wife's activities; it kept her busy and out of his hair often enough. She knew how he felt but tolerated him as well. And now it was time she headed home to start supper.

Reaching the next street corner, Lindy, along with a few other people, paused for the inevitable "WALK" sign. She pulled off her tight right glove, and then the left.

As she did so, the glove's peeling off loosened and lifted a ring from her little finger. It fell to the ground and Lindy heard a tiny clink.

"Oh, no! Granny Dora's ring!"

It had been a bit loose since she'd had it but she liked to wear it anyway.

She looked down and saw the sewer grate just below. She sighed heavily.

"Of all the foolish things to do --!" Lindy fretted silently, her expressive reactions moving the others to notice what had happened and express their sympathy. One sweet old thing said, "Oh, I hope that wasn't your wedding ring!"

"No, it was my grandmother's ring! I've had it ever since I was married."

"Oh, that's too bad." And off she went.

Lindy Shelby stayed standing at the curb.

"Now why did that have to happen?" she pondered sadly. "I wish with all my heart it didn't go down that drain."

She bent down and took a close look, all around the ground, but -- nothing. Just filthy water flowing beneath the grate. She sighed again.

"Another fond memory washed away," she thought, and started crossing the street.

As she walked the few feet to the other side, she felt something in her left shoe. She made a face and carefully removed the shoe at the corner --

And there was the ring!

What a relief! And how lucky she was! Her wish came true!

"But then, what was that clink...?" she wondered aloud.

Well, who cared? Maybe it just took a bounce. Right into her shoe. Oh, well. As long as she had it back.

"What was that stuff on the chicken?" Ross asked, wiping his mouth.

"Tarragon. Did you like it? Wasn't it good?'

"Yeah. Good," he grunted.

"I had brunch with Dana and Tiff today," Lindy volunteered. "And Tiff showed us her Monterey pictures. You know. Lee took her there for that business trip? They spent five whole days on his boat."

Grunt.

"Oh, and something weird happened right after that. Wait till you hear this!"

"What."

"I was crossing Lake Street," she began.

"No foolin'."

"Listen! I was crossing Lake Street and -- Well, just before that, I was standing on the corner and waiting for the light to change. And I took off my gloves, and next thing I know, I heard this little clink. And I knew what it was right away; it was my ring. Granny Dora's ring."

"What a shame."

"And I'm thinking 'Oh, no! It went down the drain! There was this big drain right there --"

"The sewer grate."

"Yes! So I looked all around but I couldn't find it. I was so upset... I had that ring so long...! And now I don't have it to remind me of Granny anymore! So I give up looking and crossed the street. And as I'm walking, I feel this thing in my shoe biting into my foot!"

"The ring."

"Yes...! The ring! It was right there in my shoe!"

"Great. So you didn't lose it after all. You still got it?"

"Of course!" She raised her hand for him to see.

"Yeah, wasn't that lucky. Good work."

"But wait! I didn't tell you the best part!"

"Which was --?"

"Just when I was looking around on the sidewalk and street for it, I said to myself: "Oh, I hope it didn't go down that drain. Kinda like a wish, you know?"

"Uh huh. And then you found it."

"Right! Just after I wished it back...! Kinda..."

Ross sat back with a quick smile. "Hm! Well, that's quite a little story, Lin."

Lindy started gathering dishes and taking them to the kitchenette. Ross lit a cigarette.

"So what was the little clink you heard?"

She couldn't hear him at first with the water running, so he repeated the question.

"Oh, I don't know! Must've taken a bounce, I figured."

"Yeah..." Ross replied, remembering its value. "Pretty lucky, all right!"

"Wasn't it? And it started me remembering. About Granny Dora, how sweet and generous she was with all of us. She never forgot a birthday. Always a little something. We weren't rich by any means, of course. But always something."

Ross leaned his elbows on the table, blowing smoke. He tapped off the ash into his coffee cup, still listening for a change.

"Some little toy or book. Anything. It was always something that meant a lot to both of us later on. She's the one who gave me Miss Bessie. I told you about her."

"Your doll?"

"Yes. Miss Bessie. Just an old rag doll, but my favorite growing up."

"I'm glad I married an old-fashioned girl," he grinned at her. Lindy smiled back, straightening the tablecloth.

"You still have it?"

"Miss Bessie? No...! Wish I did. I lost it years ago. Who knows where or when! I wish I could get all my old stuff back, like the ring. I hate having pieces of my childhood missing like that...my dolls, my books...those wonderful books. I miss Granny Dora most of all."

"Sure you do. Don't blame you. But at least you got the ring back, huh?"

"Yes. Wasn't that lucky!"

***

Next morning, Ross awoke first. There was something hard pressing into the sole of his foot, hard and pointy. He tossed aside the blanket and found it was a book. An old children's book, "My Day with Aunt Lou"; he saw the cover's faded colors and crushed corners.

"What the hell is *this?*" That woke Lindy up.

"G'morning. What's the matter?"

"This." He showed her the book. "Yours, I take it."

Lindy wiped a little crust from one eye and took the book from her husband. She gasped; he looked at her.

"*I remember this! My Day with Aunt Lou!*" She opened it and examined the frontispiece. "And there's my name! It's mine, from years ago!

"Uh huh. And how about *these?*" He pointed to the half-dozen or more old kids' books at the foot of the bed.

"Oh, my God! Where'd all *these* come from?!"

"You tell *me,* hon'. You obviously brought 'em in here while I was asleep," he lowed, scratching his hip.

"I did not!"

"You *didn't*...?"

"No...!"

"Well, she may be a boring chatterbox from time to time, but Lindy's no liar," came Ross's next thought. Instead he said, "Well, *I* sure didn't...! You *sure*...? You didn't go sleepwalking and --? Maybe you don't even know you did it."

"I don't think so... I think that would've woken you up. You know you're a light sleeper."

"Yeah... Well, then it's a mystery, huh? Nothin' like a nice little mystery to start your day off with."

Ross shrugged himself out of bed and went to the bathroom while Lindy thumbed through the books.

"I can't believe it! They're *all* mine! But... Where'd they all come from? How'd they get here? This is a mystery, all right...! Ross, are you sure you're not playing a trick on me? A practical joke, kinda?"

"Who, me?" He started shaving. "Couldn't be bothered."

"Then I don't get it. *I* didn't bring them in here. *You* didn't either. So how'd this happen? What's going on here?" He was amused by now.

60

"Maybe you *wished* 'em here, Lin. Y'know, wished 'em back like you did that ring?"

Lindy was thinking, didn't answer.

"Were they up in the attic?"

"What attic?"

"Doesn't this building have an attic, or basement? You coulda gone there in your sleep --"

"I *didn't,* Ross! I slept right through...! Well, now I think I'm remembering I had this dream --"

"Aha!"

"What 'aha'? No 'aha'. I am *not* a sleepwalker!"

"Looks to me like *somebody* is...!" he said, emerging to get dressed.

"Aren't you going to shower?"

"Later. At the gym."

"Oh, you're going today?"

"Yeah, me and the guys want to get in a little handball."

"When?"

"After work. Hour and half, two hours. You don't mind, do you?"

"'Course not..." She started stacking the books in her lap. "I just can't figure out how these books... Did you notice how they're all, like, water-damaged or something?"

61

"Yeah, I saw that…washed-out colors, warped pages…"

"Well, what do you think?"

Ross pulled on a shirt. "I think they got that way over the years you had 'em stashed away somewhere."

Lindy opened her mouth in protest.

"I know… You didn't. And you're not a sleepwalker. And neither am I. So, I don't know! You said you had a dream. Maybe you *dreamed* them back! Otherwise, it *is* a mystery!"

"Now you've got me thinking --"

"What?"

"Maybe there is an attic here… We used to have one on Wiswall Av'."

"Well, call me if you figure it out, hon'. Otherwise, I'd say 'Count your blessings.' Think of it as some kinda miracle!"

Lindy did think some more.

Eventually seeing Ross out the door after breakfast, Lindy made up her mind to investigate. And think some more.

***

Mrs. Shelby stood at the top of the Storage Room stairs leading to the basement. There was no attic. These stairs were dirty, dusty. No one had been down there in a year at least, she could tell.

Still, she went and asked Mr. Kallis the super. No, he didn't go moving the tenants' things around or bring them upstairs in the middle of the night. Besides, all their apartment had stowed away was that big, broken fan, a chest of drawers and some deck chairs.

"A mystery...? Or a miracle?!" she wondered on her way back upstairs now. She picked up her old books, examining them carefully.

"These books..." With her childlike scrawl in every one. Definitely hers.

"These books... smell! Ookh!! Water damage, definitely." She remembered now. When she moved from Wiswall, she had to leave some stuff behind because there was no room left in the van they rented... And it *rained heavily* all that day! And all the following week. She recalled Dana joking about their 'waterlogged honeymoon'.

So the books came from the house on Wiswall...

"So what am I -- a sleep-driver?"

***

Following dinner, Ross was getting a bit sick of all this book-mystery chatter, though he didn't want to say so. Who cares about Mr. Kallis and dusty stairs and those stupid

63

friends of hers? She was so … well, he'd put the negative aside just now.

"Look, Lindy. You wanna get to the bottom of this, test your memory or magical powers or whatnot? Okay, let's do this… Let's do a simple test. You think you may've actually dreamed these things back -- the books anyway? Not the ring."

"What kind of test?"

"Simple one. What was that doll's name? In all the old snapshots? Miss Betty?"

"Miss Bessie."

"Bessie. Right. That's been lost a long time too, right?" Lindy nodded.

"Well, then, let's do *this* -- Why don't you think about *her* tonight, all night if you want, right up to bedtime? And then --!"

"Oh, so then maybe I'll dream about her, you mean?"

"Exactly!"

"Well, I remember putting her in my Granny Dora's trunk when I was thirteen, I think. *She* had an attic."

Ross blinked slowly.

"Miss Bessie," she reminisced warmly. "I can almost feel her in my arms now…"

64

"Good, good… So, -- Pleasant dreams, Lin."

He kissed her cheek and went out to the kitchenette.

"You want a beer?" he called back.

"No… No thanks."

"Go ahead! Wish for a beer, hon'!" he kidded.

She smiled to herself, feeling sleepy already, and yawned.

***

It seemed a miracle *had* occurred. Several miracles, in fact. In two weeks' time, the Shelbys had acquired a list of items, all delivered mysteriously while they slept.

They had never seen anything materialize, but with Lindy's penchant to dream almost every night, they were never disappointed with the results.

Ross reviewed the list while they did the dishes.

"Okay, so far we got the ring, though that doesn't count. Does it?"

"Don't ask *me*…! No, that was in broad daylight."

"Anyway, the ring, the books -- six or seven kids' books."

"Seven."

"Then Miss Bessie. And Granny's cooking things. And that antique lamp. And then the big one -- the grandfather clock last night!"

"Yep. That's all so far."

"But it's *amazing,* honey! Dreaming up all these things from the past! And *then here they are,* like a time-machine delivery service or something!"

Lindy giggled, fingering the frayed edges of Miss Bessie's dress.

"I ought to put this in the wash. Or go to a dry cleaner's with her," she considered.

Ross walked over to the grandfather clock, admiring its still-handsome looks and condition.

"This was the real treasure, if you ask me. Thing must be worth about five hundred bucks!"

"It's worth more than that! Grampa George said so. He said it once belonged to one of the Roosevelts."

"Wonder what we *could* sell it for?"

"No! Don't even think about that! It isn't -- It wouldn't be right to sell any of these things now, not after -- the way they got here."

"Okay, okay...!" he appeased. "But now, instead of just cataloging our newfound wealth, let's talk more about how we can use it!"

Lindy saw a glint in his eye she didn't like.

"We've done that for two weeks now, Ross, and I say we simply --"

"And *I* say we take full advantage of this amazing new power of yours *to set us up for life!* Huh? Don'tcha think we could do that?"

"What do you mean?"

"I mean wish for money! Cash! Jewelry! Whatever turns the trick, hon'!"

"But that'd be *wrong.* That'd be stealing!"

"No, Lindy! When Granny's house was robbed five years ago, *that* was wrong! Stealing this beautiful old clock, whoever and however they did it, *that* was wrong! But it was *yours! Your* family heirloom!"

"From Grampa George's estate."

"Whatever... But can't you see what this could *do* for us?!"

"Could get us into some trouble maybe."

"*How?! Why?!* Look, we tested it, right? And we found out what works and what doesn't. The books, the doll, the clock -- They all belonged to you, right? And they all got -- wished or dreamt or *miracled* back to us, right?"

"To *me.*"

He snorted. "Same thing."

"And it's always something that was *mine,* or something I touched."

"Right. But the point is -- material things *came back...!* People, no. The kitten you had once, no. Not living things. But *things...! Things that could make us rich, honey!* Wouldn't you like to be rich?"

"Not that way."

"Why not?! Let's say you dream you've got a lot of money, precious jewels, stuff like that. *You've touched* money and jewels before, right?"

"It's wrong, Ross. It'd be wrong... I won't steal for you."
"*Steal?! Since when is dreaming stealing?!* Get your head on straight, girl!"

"We stole that grandfather clock from whoever had it last."

"A thief! We stole from a thief. So what! They had it coming! Bad karma for them, good karma for us!"

"But money -- it wouldn't be *my* money -- *our* money!"

"So what?! So somebody'd be outta pocket awhile. Plenty to go around. Maybe it'd be insured! *Diamonds* are insured!"

"*Diamonds...?!* No, Ross. I don't want diamonds."
"Well, *I* do...! I do, Lindy."

"Then go and *earn* them like other people! Don't try and make this into some -- dirty-deal master plan! I won't go along with that!"

"You won't?" he sneered.

"No. Uh-uh."

"You know, you can be *really stupid* sometimes, honey," he glared.

"Don't 'honey' me...!"

"I'll smack you one is what I'll do...!"

He raised an open palm. Lindy stepped back; this side of Ross, the angry, greedy side scared her.

"Is that what it takes to make you change your mind?!"

"No...! You're scaring me, Ross! I don't like you like this!"

"Tough! Get used to it! 'Cause if you don't agree with me on this --!"

"I'll leave you," she threatened back weakly.

"Maybe you oughta, Lindy! Or maybe *I* oughta leave!"

He swung his arm back --

Suddenly, old iron pots and pans, Granny Dora's old ones, flew out of the kitchenette and hurled themselves at Ross's head! He didn't duck in time; the frying pan beaned him, leaving a gash. He staggered in place.

Lindy Shelby retreated even more, crouching a bit.

"Who threw that god--?"

He was interrupted by the musty flurry of pages attacking his face, Lindy's old books in animated rebellion! They flapped about and slapped and poked his face and body all by themselves.

He began to lose his balance, looked down and saw Miss Bessie tightly clutching his ankles together, her wan old visage smiling up at him!

Then, the grandfather clock made a new noise... Scraping! -- Scraping slowly along the bare hallway floor. It was moving, sidling, inching its way towards Ross.

Lindy couldn't help but notice. Her hand went to her lips.

"Wha--?!" said Ross.

All at once, the outsized timepiece suddenly pitched forward.

Ross yelped with surprise.

It fell against him with a clangorous crash, its considerable weight crushing him down flat on his back at Lindy's feet and pinning him to the carpet!

"What the hell --?!" Ross Shelby managed to cry as he struggled beneath it.

"That was six months ago," Lindy thought aloud. As Dana took the rolls from their waitress, Tiff noticed Lindy smiling.

"So now you've got a whole new life ahead of you, huh, girl? How does it feel?" she asked, tasting her soup.

"Fantastic..."

"Do you miss him?" asked Dana.

"Not really. Not much. That part of my life is all in the past now..."

The Man With The Beaver Hat

Nathan was exhausted. He'd been busy all day sorting and bending and boxing and carrying and loading. His back ached, his brain fuzzy from lack of nutrition since morning.

He sure could use the fifty bucks he'd be pocketing, but he was really there because Sherilyn asked him. He wasn't about to say no to her!! They shared two classes, and he'd had his eye on her often enough for everyone to notice - especially since Professor Gunther had chastised him for 'ogling' his 'fellow students'. So no one was surprised when he volunteered to help clean out the old lady's house.

She was fetching, as Grandpa would say. Cheerleader in high school, Miss Statewide-Something-Or-Other two years ago. And he, a skinny, mop-haired sophomore film major, had been a dark horse as her potential date. But he was in there trying.

"You look wiped," Sherilyn informed him. "We need something to eat. How about you, Harriman? You hungry?"

They all called each other by their last names, like Gunther did in class.

Nathan smiled sleepily at her. "Not really. What I need is a little shut-eye, as Grandpa would say."

"Aw, come on. We're all going!"

"Yahh, you go," Nathan yawned. "I wanna just curl up right here."

"Why don't you just go home then?" suggested Kirchenbauer.

"Too far...! 'S okay. Just wake me up, or I'll hear ya when you come back."

"Can we get you something? A hamburger? Salad?"

"Yah, get me a Hamburger Salad. Perfect."

Ah, there! He finally made her laugh.

He gently settled into the expanse of quilts to be folded and boxed.

"You won't be able to sleep tonight."

"Don't bet on it."

"Well, don't sleep *there!* Those things are *filthy!*"

"No, they're just a little musty. 'S okay."

Sherilyn tugged at her hip. "They're going to the dry cleaners."

Nathan half-buried his face into warm, plush folds.

"Just throw me in with 'em..."

They left about ten-thirty.

Nathan Harriman cuddled comfortably. His mind traveled from the landscaping he'd done yesterday to Sherilyn... Then to her late aunt, the one who'd lived so long

75

alone, the former silent movie actress whose belongings they'd been removing room by room in that huge suburban palace. Part turn-of-the-century mansion, part film museum it was. He recalled Sherry saying there's no telling what treasures might be found within.

She'd worked with many famous stars of her day, and had amassed so much to prove and commemorate that. He'd have to google some of those names on the wall photos. Who was Conrad Nagel? Billy Bitzer? William Beaudine? Lucille LaVerne?

Next minute, he was asleep, and dreaming...

What was that? A garish, unsmiling clown stood beneath a full moon and turned to face him...

Then he was indoors, a dark place with cobwebs almost everywhere. On furniture, on the staircase, on the suit of armor, dust and cobwebs.

He noticed ancient, tatty drapes hung and collapsed onto the floors as he walked through the parlor.

'Not suicide,' he heard someone say in a stern baritone, and then: 'Smithson!'.

Who was Smithson? He'd have to google her... *'Her'*? Somehow he knew Smithson was a woman.

There was an older man wearing those squeeze-on

glasses with a ribbon. Like in the old movies.

And others. How could Nathan know their names? But he did. There was Miss Smithson, who looked like a plump goose, Professor Burke with the glasses, Lucille, the stately beauty, Sir James, that very concerned, elderly gent and young Arthur Hibbs. *Who were these people and how did he know them?!*

"I can prove it wasn't suicide," the Professor intoned. But oddly, Nathan couldn't actually hear his voice. He just knew what he was saying, what everybody was thinking and saying.

They all ascended the stairs to a room adorned with a wreath and a sword through the center of it. The door opened, revealing a lady's *boudoir*, one that'd been the scene of a messy struggle. Things scattered, floral-patterned chairs rested face-down and on their sides.

Outdoors, an owl silently hooted, and observed.

Through French doors, the figure of another young woman stood and raised her arms; she had artificial bat-wings made of gauze webbing her arms to her sides! She snarled at the party gathered with dark teeth.

Smithson gave a noiseless shriek.

Nathan shuddered. If that wasn't a vampire --?!

"Luna!" gasped Nathan in his sleep. He even knew *her* name! *How?!*

Sir James seemed agitated, the Professor cautious and philosophical.

"They sleep in spots accursed," the latter said wordlessly. Nathan had read that somewhere, he was sure...

And he was equally certain that a man named Roger Balfour was still alive. 'Not a suicide.' -- Was that him?

Luna's dead, eager face loomed closer behind the cobwebs...

Then -- *he* was there!

He wore a tall beaver hat and cloak. He walked with purpose in an almost-comical crouch. But the face was by no means comical; it was hideous! Long, straggling hair cascaded down the sides of a face truly from Hell! Eyes forced open wider-than-wide, unable to blink away the horrors they'd seen. A lipless mouth baring sharpened teeth above and below! A motionless, horrible face staring, hands beckoning to him. He had bat-wings too!

Nathan felt cold sweat beading his brow and neck and palms.

The Man with the Beaver Hat now "spoke", now gesturing in a new direction.

"Beneath the staircase," the apparition indicated urgently.

"You will find it there...! Find it there, find it there...!"

78

Sherilyn, Kirchenbauer and the others returned noisily, chatting and rattling paper fast-food bags. Nathan's eyes popped open.

"Have a nice nap?" his crush wanted to know.

"No... I mean, i don't know. I had a dream, almost like a nightmare, but more like -- I dunno. It was like *déja vu*, y'know? All kinda familiar in a weird way."

Sherilyn and some others ate while listening. Harriman described in detail what he'd seen and heard in his slumber, then asked: "Any of that make sense to you, Sher'?"

"Yeah, it does! You just ran that film we read about for Gunther in your mind! Don't you remember?"

"You mean that --? Of course! Yah, that's it!"

"All that stuff was in there," Kirchenbauer added. "The names, the sets, the dialogue from the title cards... Right, Sher'? All except --"

"Except what?"

"Well, it's a *lost* film, remember?" Sherilyn reminded them. "And that last part wasn't in the movie. The part about 'beneath the staircase' and 'Find it there'. Have any of you been under there yet?"

No, no one had.

"I wonder," she paused before standing. "Let's go look!"

They all went and looked.   Sherilyn stopped Kirchenbauer from going in first.

"Let Harriman look. It was his dream!"

So Nathan Harriman looked…

And that's how the reels of the most sought-after lost silent film in history were rediscovered.

The Man with the Beaver Hat would've been proud of his work.

****

The
Trick
and
The
Treat

Hallowe'en again, and the little ones would soon be at her door. She not only didn't mind, she always looked forward to it, though it was rather tiring just going to the door.

Oh, well, it was only once a year, and this year she had the bright idea of stationing herself just inside the door. She walked minimally now; last March, she'd had to acquire two canes to assist her moving about the house.

Addie Filkins felt she was falling apart bit by bit. She could recite in great detail all the things she used to be able to do - and did, but couldn't do anymore. By herself, that is.

Not that Addie Filkins was ever helpless. No, she'd never been bad off as all that. She could still function. All it took was a little extra effort...

She wondered how many innocent, piping voices this season would ask: "Are you a witch?"

She always answered, "Well, it's Hallowe'en night, so maybe I am! *Do you think I'm a witch?*"

And was always amused by their reactions.

Now she spied a small group across the street: hobo, super-hero, girl tiger, princess and clown. Average age: ten. They'd be here shortly.

Her treats were ready, in the big bowl on the antique cherrywood table next to the door: small fruits and nuts in one hundred chocolates she dipped and wrapped herself every year. One of her holiday hobbies.

It wasn't long before the doorbell rang. Addie donned her glasses and hearing aid and adjusted her wig...

She closed the door after the cute teenage Cleopatra and scarecrow's departure and checked the time. "As late as that?"

Again, it had been a fun way to spend the evening, she thought. No doubt Hallowe'en was Addie Filkins' favorite holiday. It used to be Christmas or Thanksgiving, but not since her family and friends either died or moved away.

So another few pleasant hours had passed, chatting with and treating all those eager youngsters wearing costumes she couldn't identify. She'd often ask who they were supposed to be to keep them with her a little longer. She felt young again through them, she knew.

Sometimes she'd talk to their parents, informing them that her treats were home-made (which most of them already knew, having been former visitors themselves).

Addie looked at her treat bowl: only five left.

Lightly, she sighed.

Just about bedtime anyway.

Then, the doorbell again. She looked at her watch. Not too late for a straggler.

She stood without her canes and opened the door. There stood a splendidly attired boy magician, about twelve, with lank, dark hair under his topper, penciled mustache and domino mask, wielding a plastic magic wand.

"Trick or treat, young lady!"

Addie laughed and said: "I do believe that's the best outfit I've seen tonight! And what's your name? Merlin, perhaps?"

"I am Barvelli the Mystifying...! My real name's Barry Covelli so I just put 'em together and - Presto!"

"Barvelli! What an imagination you have!"

"Yes, ma'am. A good magician needs one."

Addie smiled sweetly at the charming lad.

"Are you a real magician?"

"I sure am! I can do eighty-eight tricks!"

"Well, don't let me keep you waiting. Here you are!" And she reached into the bowl and dropped the five remaining chocolates into his bag.

"Thank you, Ma'am... Would you like to see a trick?"

Slightly startled, Addie Filkins reset her hearing aid plug, inquiring: "Eh? You want to show me a trick? Why, I'd be delighted!"

84

Displaying both sides of his hands, Barvelli began: "Then direct your eyes *here*, young lady, and notice that at no time do my fingers leave my hands!"

"That's an old joke for such a young fellow!" Addie chuckled.

"It was in the book. *Watch!*"

Next, traditional tiny white balls appeared between his fingers, first five, then with a practiced flourish, one less with each pass until --

"The Great Barvelli! Wonderful!" Addie applauded.

"'Barvelli the *Mystifying!*' if you please." he cheerily corrected.

"Yes, of course. 'The Mystifying'... Now... would *you* like to see a trick?"

Barry grinned a tad skeptically. "*You* do magic tricks?"

"Well, I'll do just one. But it's a good one! Want to see it?"

"Uh sure!"

"Then just a second while I prepare."

The feeble little old lady removed some hairpins, let her hearing aid plug dangle, set her glasses on the tip of her nose and loosened her full set of dentures.

"Ready?" she prompted.

"Yes, ma'am…" Barry felt his innards lurch warily.

"Say the magic words!"

"Wha- What magic words?"

"Sassafras tea!"

No turning back now. "Sassafras tea!"

Addie Filkins then bent down a little and hobbled back a few steps, just enough to leave her wig, glasses and false teeth suspended in mid-air!

Barvelli the Mystifying leapt back a foot, transfixed!

Next, the dangling ear-plug rose to face-level and her two canes started thumping towards them from across the foyer!

The boy scooted down the pathway and street at top speed, leaving Addie cackling merrily just inside her front door.

"Oh, but I do love trick-or-treat!"

She summoned the canes to follow, and toddled off to the stairlift, her wig and sensory apparatuses leading the way.

****

Holy
Terror

It might have been a sad occasion. Or one of sympathy and comfort. But naturally, Verna Goodfriend made that impossible.

"No consideration, that's what I get. That's my reward for trying to bring you up right... Did I get any help from your father?"

Charles tried to break in.

"No. Never any help from *him!* *Ask* him...! No help from anyone."

No one cared to remind her that Stanley had passed.

"I had to do it all myself! And *you* didn't make it easy! Oh, no! Nothing but trouble, the bunch of you!" With pursed lips, she turned her head on the pillow.

Valerie leaned in a bit and, adjusting the thin blue blanket, said: "Try to rest, Mother."

"*'Rest'?!* Hah! That's good coming from you!" Mother Verna spewed. "My needy, greedy daughter-in-law who can't wait for me to go to my final reward so she and Chester can spend what little I have left on themselves and their ungrateful brats! Take your hands off of me!"

Chester pulled her back by the arm while his wife wisely kept her mouth closed. The kids shuffled their feet, hating every moment of this and all wishing to be elsewhere.

Charles and Virginia felt that way too. But Mother Verna was dying, all the doctors told them. There was no more hope for recovery.

So this gathering had been inevitable, and just as miserable an occasion as they'd imagined, but still necessary. And they truly did feel remorse for the inevitable, but knew a growing sense of relief awaited it.

"Yes, you scruffy, thankless, nasty little brats -- There's no other word for you. Did you ever send me a birthday card? Or a Christmas card? Anything? No. The lot of you. Ethan, Jennifer, Toby."

Now Charles spoke: "F'gosh sakes, Mom! Toby's three years old!"

"I don't care. Ungrateful, that's what you are, all of you. Leave me alone now."

"All right, Mother," volunteered Virginia. "But remember we all love you. Even if we're not all perfect."

"You certainly aren't! And whose fault is that?!"

The Goodfriends retreated from the bedroom that looked more like a hospital room to the parlor. Dr. Hartnell, that good family friend, was still standing by.

Ethan felt hungry and helped himself to a sandwich. His Dad Chester was hungry too, but thought about having a drink instead. He told his son not to eat too much. Chester and Virginia spoke with the doctor about her refusal to consider home care, even a nurse.

She was quite a problem as a patient all these years, no one was surprised to learn. She'd even threatened to sue her physician many times over the years.

It was all the family could do to get Mother Verna to prepare her estate without making trouble.

"I'll show you how things ought to be done!" she'd railed, bullying them all, even the attorneys.

Verna Goodfriend died that night at age eighty-six. Her wake and funeral were well-attended. Her family hoped she'd be happy now...

"I'm extremely sorry, Mrs. Goodfriend, but although you never did anything during your lifetime to warrant eternal damnation, you *must* spend *some* time in Purgatory for giving everyone down there such a hard time!"

"*Oh?! Is that so?!*"

"Let go of my ear, Mrs. Goodfriend! Please!"

"*Open that gate!* I *demand* to see the Management! Who made *you* a saint anyway?!"

Toupee

or

Not

Toupee

It was a bad dream, I think... I couldn't remember much of it when I woke up. In retrospect, though, I'd have to say it was exciting. All that stayed with me was the feeling that I was floating, neither up nor down, but just floating. What's exciting about that, I really don't know. But that's just the way the day began. That's the only thing that happened that morning, or the night before, that I could call even a bit unusual.

Otherwise, everything was normal. My bathroom routine was uneventful. I remember shaving and putting on after-shave. So I did see myself in the mirror.

Absolutely nothing unusual.

I left for work, got in the car and onto the main highway, like always. I put on the radio, listened to the news, the helicopter traffic guy and the weather.

I get off at my ramp and do the three side streets to the place I work, Security Mutual.

I ring for the elevator at the basement parking level. I wait around for a minute. A couple of three people from another department come over. They're waiting with me. I take off my hat and wipe my hand over my scalp.

"Hot already," I thought to myself. "Glad I got in early today."

We get in the elevator and punch our buttons. Then one of them, a woman, starts to look at me funny. Like I did something weird. I ignored her and waited for my floor.

I got off at my floor, which is Six, in case you're interested. The staring lady and the other people had pressed Eight. I walked to my desk, tossed my hat over the lamp that I never use, as a lamp anyway. Then I go over to the kitchen and grab my personal mug. We all have our own that we keep there. The coffee's still brewing, so I wash my hands. And in comes Norma, who I think is beautiful.

I look over at her and smile. And I'm surprised to see she's looking at me like she never did before! Like the elevator lady, only friendlier.

I felt very self-conscious. I wondered what was up. 'Cause I'm early? Is my fly down? What the heck is going on? I can't understand it, you know?

So I'm drying my hands while we're waiting for the coffee, and she says:

"Good morning, Ken!" And her voice is different, like she's pleased about something. I notice this right away. Well, this lady I can't ignore. So I say:

"Good morning. What's new?"

And she laughs. And then she says, *"You* tell *me!"*

But I can't think of anything new, and now I'm feeling a little self-conscious.

"Well, let me tell *you*, then!" She crosses her arms. "It's about time, I think!"

I nod like I know what the heck she's talking about, but I don't, so I wait for her to finish.

"It's perfect! You made a wise decision," she makes up her mind with this cute little nod. And smiles at me again like she's never seen me before.

I'm confused now. I'm tongue-tied, you know? So I still don't say anything at first, then I had to.

"What the heck are you talking about?" I ask nicely.

She blushes a little.

"Well, Ken...! It won't be much of a secret! Not to *us*, anyway! But your new customers will never guess, I'm sure!"

"About what?!" I almost want to yell, but she goes on talking. And I can't help but listen because I really like her.

"Wait till Mrs. Beeble sees it! I shouldn't tell you, but she always said how much better you'd look if you got one! And now you did! Well, congratulations. I think you did right by yourself."

And with that, she comes over to the coffee urn...where I'm standing... and she's really taking a good look at my head now, and I'm ready to take off out the door! Pretty as she is, and as much as I always wanted some extra attention from her, you know...I wasn't expecting *this!*

"Just perfect," she says now, and gets herself some coffee. Then she walks to the open doorway. "I can't wait to see the reactions!" she says. And then she leaves.

Coffee? I need a drink! 'Cause I'm wracking my brain now, trying to figure out what brought all this on. So I get my coffee and go to the door.

And I stop. Half the office is there. And they're all looking at me and smiling! Norma again too. Mrs. Beeble looks like she's looking at a new baby, cooing, all coy and flustery. I was starting to get a little scared!

Maybe I should back up a little more. 'Cause I don't think I mentioned -- I'm bald. Very little up there. Just like my uncles. On my mother's side. Right after high school, just before I started that job is when my crowning glory started deserting me. So, all the months and years I've worked at Security Mutual, I Was a Teenage Cue Ball, you know?

The hat I wear, by the way, is the one I inherited from my father. You know, the guy with all the hair in the picture on my desk. I wear it for -- Well, let's call it good luck.

Do you think this might be significant? Some do. Now.

Anyway, so that's who I was. The guy I shaved that morning. But this wasn't the same guy they were looking at now. Everybody thought I looked great! Better, somehow.

It took me *that long* before it dawned on me -- They were acting as if I was wearing a toupee!

This really amused me and I burst out in laughter.

I said: "Whoa! Talk about your *subtle hints --!*"

I thought they were kidding! Did they buy me one as a gift?!

But all they kept saying was what a good idea it was. For me to *get one --* no, *to have gotten one --!* And such a perfect one, too!

I laughed really hard and I went to the nearest mirror, thinking: 'Ha ha. This is a good one on me.' Real bitterly, you know?

And then, when I came to the mirror and looked in it, I saw--! – Nothing!

And I had to laugh again!

Were they all *crazy?* Or was it *me* now? After all the years of sameness...

But they seemed to insist, all these sincere people, that they saw me in a toupee.

But, as I just told you, I saw nothing up there. I broke out in a cold sweat and excused myself fast. I ran to the Men's Room and splashed cold water in my face and looked at myself. I felt the scalp. Now I saw and *felt* nothing... I didn't get the joke.

But they never acted like it was a joke. It was like a scene from a play. You know what I mean? I was out of sync! I was in the Twilight Zone! The *old* version! I thought maybe I had gone crazy.

But then, I started to play along, just to see what would happen.

What happened was I was treated with a new respect. Somehow, that was even more surprising to me -- then.

The day went by just fine, with me acknowledging their compliments, and nobody had any trouble keeping a straight face.

I said to myself: "All right, then, go with it! Better to play along than admit you're deranged."

I didn't have trouble sleeping. I just nodded off while I was thinking, lying on my couch. No dreams, though.

But the next day, the same thing...

"They sure can keep a straight face," I thought. "But when is the joke going to end?" You know?

Well, that was three weeks ago. And since that time, my sales went up twelve percent. The customers liked my 'young ideas'. It's true that when I *did* have hair, I had this boyish look.

Now, the very next thing I know -- I'm up on twelve in the boss's office, being commended and given a new title. With less paperwork and a ten percent raise. Now I'm a District Manager. And they're all proud of me.

Me and my perfect toupee.

Invisible, yes, but only to the wearer! I'm still wearing my father's hat, by the way. But now for the reason that maybe it brought me some luck after all.

And what else? Oh. Norma and I are dating. And this is fine with me. 'Cause I figured: 'What the heck. Why make a fuss about this?' You know?

Though now, for the past few days, they've all starting looking at me funny, like the elevator lady.

And Norma just told me it's because -- now I need a haircut.

****

Daughter

of

Memory

Wait. Wait, and you will see.

See what I see.

Wait. And you will see *her*.

She's always there.

Whenever I wish. Whenever she wished --

She will always be there.

I don't know who she is -- or was. There is no name, never a name for her. This too is constant, as constant as she is pervasive.

But she's always there, always there, somewhere within.

Up there.

No, I am not joking. I couldn't, not about her, not this girl. I promise you.

And I promise you she will be here, presently, not impossibly, flickering through the past into our view.

Up there.

You'll see her, I know. I promise you. I promise.

She has promised *me*, in a way.

And changed me.

As she will change you.

For the more I have looked, the more I have seen. And the more I see, the more I see her. Always, always... her.

Don't look away now. And not at me. Keep looking. You'll see. She'll be here... any moment.

Haunting, this girl. A wisp of a thing, a will-o'-the-wisp perhaps. You'll know her when you see her.

Beautiful? Pretty? Both.

Young and old.

Happy and sad.

Invisible, irresistible.

She's in everything. Everything.

In this too, yes.

You've seen her already, a hundred times!

But you must look again. To *really* see her.

Look and you will find her, always there, and it will seem to be for the first time.

You'll see... You'll see her.

She is inevitable. Inescapable. Necessary.

I have seen her walk in shadows, and through them, and with them, a shadow herself.

There is no name, no word for her presence.

But *what* presence...!

Omnipresence: that's what she is!

And versatile? Yes, always...

She may be the slave girl, one of many, suffering, writhing. Or the country maid, blissful and serene. Or she is now the vampire, dark-eyed, gaunt and coiled. The flower girl, flirt or flapper, stylish, oh-so-smart and winking -- winking at me -- *for* me. Beckoning, daring...

Soon she'll be here with us. Watch and see.

I've studied this, studied and found her. *I* found her.

In every work, in everything!

The discovery of her was breathtaking. Every time, every place, she was there. *Is* there.

Never so grand, so major an impression. But small, elusive, coaxing one to find her.

And once found, always there.

And now she's mine.

But not just mine. She's greater than that. More than that. As you will see.

And when you see, she'll be *yours* as well.

Keep looking. Keep watching.

Soon, soon...

Now!

There!

See her moving! Drifting! See her now!

See her love pour forth...! Ah, radiance! Shine for us!

Now drift -- but slowly! -- across the plane of grey time, O silent beauty on high, out of our subconscious, into our present, into our eyes and minds and souls!

Yes, you see her now.

And now, forever!

She is the waif this time, the street girl. See her plead! Eyes wide, unblinking, enhanced by black. A moving picture, this girl, this slip of a thing, this daughter of memory.

Yes, she makes us cry, for sheer loveliness alone!

O, girl! Stay for us! Drift and flicker, but stay! Kindly stay this time!

No, don't vanish again! Be with us longer! Stay! Stay...

But -- gone now, yes. Gone again, this girl. Gone again, already.

Substanceless, soundless, she's wafted away... as intangibly, as cruelly as she came.

And did you see her...?

Yes. And --

Did she see *us?*

We can never know.

She will not speak.

Teasing girl! Heartless girl! Again you thwart our finest dreams! You, who are a dream yourself, never stay. Never stay.

Why, then, do you ever appear?! What torture is this... that you will never, never obey?! You never satisfy your lovers, we who always attend! You never stay, never abide.

We want you.

But you never want us, never enough to stay.

We love you.

Yet you will never love us, not ever.

Silver wraith of light and darkness, creature of dust long blown beyond, the Muse of emulsion you are.

You are in everything. But nothing more than the mind.

So we will wait.

And you will come again to us, the speechless, eldritch actress, maker of gestures, the presence that always will linger and never remain.

So *we* must remain, to continue, then, now and always, to watch, to wait, to waver in half-light, to only be with you.

So that never need we ask...

When shall I see you again?

****

About The Author

Emmy Award Winner Joe Alaskey, whose Internet Movie Database page and resume reads like a *Who's Who* of Hollywood, has enjoyed an illustrious career as one of the most sought-after voice over artists in the TV and Film industry, as well as memorable performances as an actor for Film, TV, Radio and Stage.

A theatrical veteran and comedy circuit regular, Joe Alaskey was plucked from the stage and comedy clubs in the 80s to star in the feature film *Lucky Stiff*, directed by Anthony Perkins, and won a place in the hearts of millions as the lovable Uncle Beano on the science fiction situation comedy, *Out of This World*. A fixture on 80s television, he was the co-star of *Couch Potatoes* and guest starred on countless shows including *Head of the Class*, *Night Court*, *Hollywood Squares* and *The Match Game*.

Referred to by fans as "The Man of a Million Voices," Joe Alaskey took the animation world by storm voicing hundreds of animation projects including *The Looney Tunes*, *Tiny Toon Adventures*, *Duck Dodgers*, *Rugrats*, *All Grown Up*, *Tom & Jerry*, and too many others to list. Joe Alaskey has written stage plays and radio scripts, as well as *The Wild, Wild West Show* for Six Flags Over Texas. Joe Alaskey is the best-selling author of *That's Still Not All, Folks!!* (Bear Manor Media) and currently performs as the voice of the narrator on the television series *Murder Comes To Town* for the Investigation Discovery Network.

About The Editors

K.P. Lynne & R.J. Modell are best-selling authors, bloggers, social media writers, poets, song lyricists, playwrights and business writers. They enjoy writing stories for kids, teens and adults. Together they wrote the children's book, *Hock E. Puck Meets Hock E. Stick,* which was a #1 Hot New Release for six weeks and a Top 5 best-selling eBook and print book.

R.J. Modell and K.P. Lynne are members of the Chicago Writers Association and serve as Illinois Reads Ambassadors for the Illinois Reading Council.

K.P. Lynne earned a *Young Author Award* and wrote the best-selling books *Litty Kitter the Cat, the E-Z Reads Edition* and *Litty Kitter Is Kitty Litter Spelled Backwards.* R.J. Modell was honored with a *Writers Making Things Write Award.*

Together, R.J. Modell & K.P. Lynne have touched millions of people's lives with their poems, quotes and words of wisdom via social media and their healing words have been donated on postcards to veterans, senior citizens and hospitals.

K.P. Lynne and R.J. Modell enjoy using their talents and gifts to help others and do extensive volunteer work. Visit their websites at www.RJModell.com and www.KPLynne.com.

Find them on Facebook at Facebook.com/RJModell and Facebook.com/KPLynneFanPage.

Social Media Links

Facebook.com/JoeAlaskeyFans
Facebook.com/QueasyStreet

Facebook.com/KPLynneFanPage
Facebook.com/RJModell

Twitter.com/JoeAlaskey
Twitter.com/QueasyStreetJoe

Twitter.com/KPLynne
Twitter.com/RJModell

Queasy Street Fan Shop
Powered By Café Press

CafePress.com/QueasyStreet

Be The Envy of Your Street!!
Wear Official Queasy Street Gear!!

Get Your Queasy Street
T-Shirt, Hoodie
or
Book Bag Today!!

www.ingramcontent.com/pod-product-compliance
Lightning Source LLC
Chambersburg PA
CBHW070344130626

46556CB00007B/3025